WOULD YOU RATHER?

7 YEAR OLD
VERSION

FOLLOW US AT:

 WWW.FACEBOOK.COM/
WOULDYOURATHERBOOK

 @WOULDYOURATHERBOOK

WWW.WOULDYOURATHERBOOK.COM

COME
JOIN OUR GROUP

GET A BONUS PDF PACKED WITH HILARIOUS JOKES, AND THINGS TO MAKE YOU SMILE!

GO TO:

shorturl.at/cdLRT

■ **Get a Bonus fun PDF** (filled with jokes, and fun would you rather questions)

■ **Get entered into our monthly competition to win a $100 Amazon gift card**

■ **Hear about our up and coming new books**

HOW TO PLAY?

You can play to win or play for fun, the choice is yours!

1. Player 1 asks player 2 to either choose questions **A** or **B**.

2. Then player 1 reads out the chosen questions.

3. Player 2 decides on an answer to their dilemma, and either memorize their answer or notes it down.

4. Player 1 has to guess player 2's answer. If they guess correctly they win a point, if not player 2 wins a point.

5. Take turns asking the questions, **the first to 7 points wins.**

Note: IT CAN BE FUN TO DO FUNNY VOICES OR MAKE SILLY FACES

REMEMBER
Do **NOT** ATTEMPT TO DO ANY OF THE SCENARIOS IN THIS BOOK, THEY ARE ONLY MEANT FOR FUN!

WOULD YOU RATHER?

7 YEAR OLD
VERSION

PLAYER 1

(ASK THE OTHER PLAYER(S) TO
CHOOSE QUESTION 1 OR QUESTION 2)

WOULD YOU RATHER

BE ABLE TO MAKE IT
RAIN MONEY

 OR

HAVE A MONEY TREE IN
YOUR GARDEN?

WOULD YOU RATHER

GO TO A RESTAURANT ON
THE MOON

 OR

THE BOTTOM OF THE
OCEAN?

WOULD YOU RATHER?

7 YEAR OLD
VERSION

PLAYER 2

(ASK THE OTHER PLAYER(S) TO
CHOOSE QUESTION 1 OR QUESTION 2)

A

WOULD YOU RATHER

HAVE THE CHANCE TO RIDE AN ELEPHANT

 OR

A CAMEL TO SCHOOL?

B

WOULD YOU RATHER

MOO WHEN YOU COUGH

 OR

NEIGH WHEN YOU HICCUP?

WOULD YOU RATHER?

7 YEAR OLD
VERSION

PLAYER 1

(ASK THE OTHER PLAYER(S) TO
CHOOSE QUESTION 1 OR QUESTION 2)

A

WOULD YOU RATHER

HAVE EYE ON THE BACK OF YOUR HEAD

 OR

ON THE SIDE OF YOUR HEAD?

B

WOULD YOU RATHER

BE GIVEN THE ABILITY TO READ YOUR CLASSMATES' MINDS

 OR

BE INVISIBLE AT SCHOOL?

WOULD YOU RATHER?

7 YEAR OLD
VERSION

PLAYER 2

(ASK THE OTHER PLAYER(S) TO
CHOOSE QUESTION 1 OR QUESTION 2)

A

WOULD YOU RATHER

HAVE A LONGER
LUNCHTIME AT SCHOOL
BUT HAVE TO EAT
VEGETABLES

HAVE A SHORTER
LUNCHTIME BUT EAT
NOTHING BUT CANDY?

B

WOULD YOU RATHER

ONLY BE ABLE TO SIT

ONLY BE ABLE TO STAND?

WOULD YOU RATHER?

7 YEAR OLD
VERSION

PLAYER 1

(ASK THE OTHER PLAYER(S) TO
CHOOSE QUESTION 1 OR QUESTION 2)

A

WOULD YOU RATHER

HAVE MORE SHORT SCHOOL HOLIDAYS DURING THE YEAR

LESS BUT LONGER ONES?

B

WOULD YOU RATHER

LIVE TO BE 300 YEARS OLD

LIVE A NORMAL LENGTH WITH SUPER STRENGTH?

WOULD YOU RATHER?

7 YEAR OLD
VERSION

PLAYER 2

(ASK THE OTHER PLAYER(S) TO
CHOOSE QUESTION 1 OR QUESTION 2)

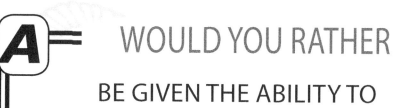

A

WOULD YOU RATHER

BE GIVEN THE ABILITY TO NEVER GET SICK AGAIN

 OR

NEVER GET INJURED AGAIN?

B

WOULD YOU RATHER

BE REALLY GOOD AT MATHS

 OR

BE REALLY GOOD AT ART?

WOULD YOU RATHER?

7 YEAR OLD
VERSION

PLAYER 1

(ASK THE OTHER PLAYER(S) TO
CHOOSE QUESTION 1 OR QUESTION 2)

A — WOULD YOU RATHER

NEVER STOP SPEAKING

NEVER BE ABLE TO
SPEAK AGAIN?

B — WOULD YOU RATHER

HAVE FEET WHERE YOUR
HANDS SHOULD BE

HANDS WHERE YOUR
FEET SHOULD BE?

WOULD YOU RATHER?

7 YEAR OLD
VERSION

PLAYER 2

(ASK THE OTHER PLAYER(S) TO
CHOOSE QUESTION 1 OR QUESTION 2)

WOULD YOU RATHER

A

BETURNED INTO A CAT

OR

A DOG?

WOULD YOU RATHER

B

HAVE LOTS OF BROTHERS AND SISTERS

OR

NO BROTHERS AND SISTERS?

WOULD YOU RATHER?

7 YEAR OLD
VERSION

PLAYER 1

(ASK THE OTHER PLAYER(S) TO
CHOOSE QUESTION 1 OR QUESTION 2)

A

WOULD YOU RATHER

HAVE A REMOTE-CONTROLLED BOAT

 OR

A REMOTE-CONTROLLED PLANE?

B

WOULD YOU RATHER

HAVE TO ALWAYS READ AT LEAST ONE BOOK A WEEK

 OR

NEVER READ A BOOK AGAIN?

WOULD YOU RATHER?

7 YEAR OLD
VERSION

PLAYER 2

(ASK THE OTHER PLAYER(S) TO
CHOOSE QUESTION 1 OR QUESTION 2)

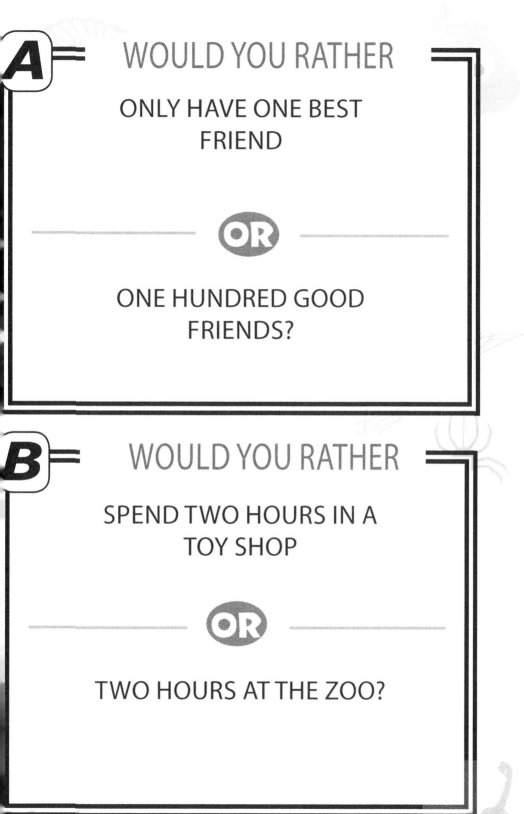

A

WOULD YOU RATHER

ONLY HAVE ONE BEST FRIEND

OR

ONE HUNDRED GOOD FRIENDS?

B

WOULD YOU RATHER

SPEND TWO HOURS IN A TOY SHOP

OR

TWO HOURS AT THE ZOO?

WOULD YOU RATHER?

7 YEAR OLD
VERSION

PLAYER 1

(ASK THE OTHER PLAYER(S) TO
CHOOSE QUESTION 1 OR QUESTION 2)

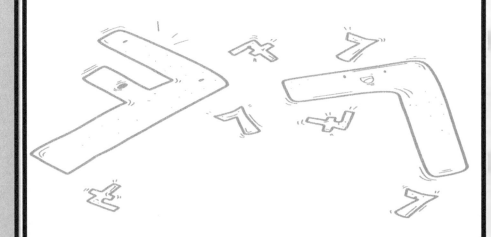

A

WOULD YOU RATHER

ONLY WATCH TV SHOWS

 OR

MOVIES?

B

WOULD YOU RATHER

BE ABLE TO STAY THE AGE YOU ARE FOR THE REST OF YOUR LIFE

 OR

BE A GROWN-UP RIGHT AWAY?

WOULD YOU RATHER?

7 YEAR OLD
VERSION

PLAYER 2

(ASK THE OTHER PLAYER(S) TO
CHOOSE QUESTION 1 OR QUESTION 2)

A

WOULD YOU RATHER

GET TAKEN FOR A RIDE IN A POLICE CAR

 OR

A FIRE TRUCK?

B

WOULD YOU RATHER

EAT FRIES WITH EVERY MEAL

 OR

EAT CANDY WITH EVERY MEAL?

WOULD YOU RATHER?

7 YEAR OLD
VERSION

PLAYER 1

(ASK THE OTHER PLAYER(S) TO
CHOOSE QUESTION 1 OR QUESTION 2)

A

WOULD YOU RATHER

YOU HAD TO GIVE UP WATCHING TV

OR

GIVE UP EATING JUNK FOOD?

B

WOULD YOU RATHER

MAKE A MOVIE

OR

DESIGN A TOY?

WOULD YOU RATHER?

7 YEAR OLD
VERSION

PLAYER 2

(ASK THE OTHER PLAYER(S) TO
CHOOSE QUESTION 1 OR QUESTION 2)

A

WOULD YOU RATHER

HAVE SMELLY FEET

BAD BREATH?

B

WOULD YOU RATHER

GET TO EAT THE BEST ICE
CREAM IN THE WORLD
ONCE IN YOUR LIFE

EAT GOOD ICE CREAM
ONCE A WEEK FOR THE
REST OF YOUR LIFE?

WOULD YOU RATHER?

7 YEAR OLD
VERSION

PLAYER 1

(ASK THE OTHER PLAYER(S) TO
CHOOSE QUESTION 1 OR QUESTION 2)

A

WOULD YOU RATHER

BE ROYALTY BUT NEVER SEE YOUR FAMILY AGAIN

BE POOR AND LIVE WITH YOUR FAMILY?

B

WOULD YOU RATHER

TRAIN TO BE A DOCTOR

TO BE A FIREFIGHTER?

WOULD YOU RATHER?

7 YEAR OLD
VERSION

PLAYER 2

(ASK THE OTHER PLAYER(S) TO
CHOOSE QUESTION 1 OR QUESTION 2)

WOULD YOU RATHER

BE THE FUNNIEST KID IN SCHOOL

 OR

BE THE SMARTEST KID IN SCHOOL?

WOULD YOU RATHER

BUY ONE 100 DOLLAR TOY

 OR

100 ONE DOLLAR TOYS?

WOULD YOU RATHER?

7 YEAR OLD
VERSION

PLAYER 1

(ASK THE OTHER PLAYER(S) TO
CHOOSE QUESTION 1 OR QUESTION 2)

A

WOULD YOU RATHER

YOU HAD A GIGANTIC NOSE

 OR

GIANT EARS?

B

WOULD YOU RATHER

NEVER KNOW WHAT DAY IT WAS

 OR

NEVER KNOW WHAT TIME IT WAS?

WOULD YOU RATHER?

7 YEAR OLD
VERSION

PLAYER 2

(ASK THE OTHER PLAYER(S) TO
CHOOSE QUESTION 1 OR QUESTION 2)

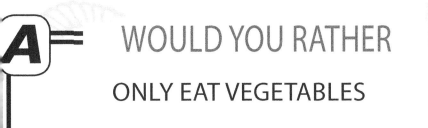

WOULD YOU RATHER

ONLY EAT VEGETABLES

 OR

ONLY EAT MEAT?

WOULD YOU RATHER

WAKE UP ONE MORNING LOST IN THE JUNGLE

 OR

LOST IN THE DESERT?

WOULD YOU RATHER?

7 YEAR OLD
VERSION

PLAYER 1

(ASK THE OTHER PLAYER(S) TO
CHOOSE QUESTION 1 OR QUESTION 2)

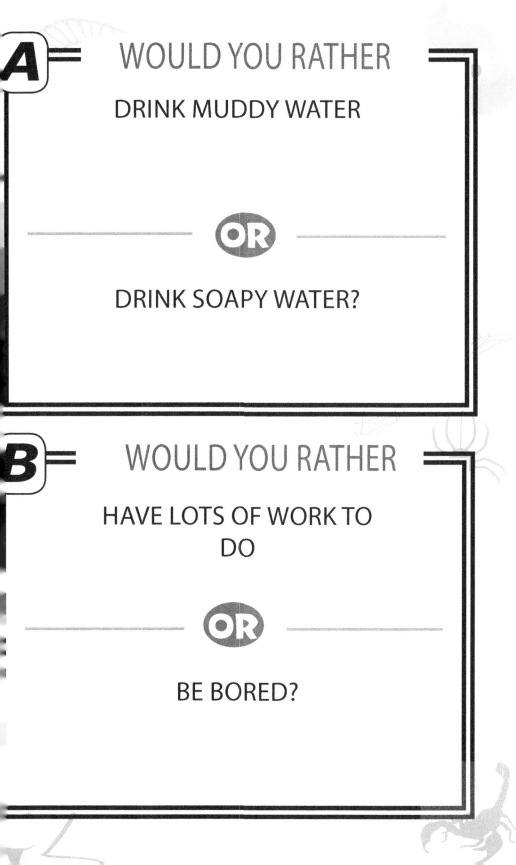

WOULD YOU RATHER

A

DRINK MUDDY WATER

OR

DRINK SOAPY WATER?

WOULD YOU RATHER

B

HAVE LOTS OF WORK TO DO

OR

BE BORED?

WOULD YOU RATHER?

7 YEAR OLD
VERSION

PLAYER 2

(ASK THE OTHER PLAYER(S) TO
CHOOSE QUESTION 1 OR QUESTION 2)

A

WOULD YOU RATHER

HAVE A HOT DRINK

 OR

A COLD DRINK?

B

WOULD YOU RATHER

WEAR SHOES THAT ARE
ONE SIZE TOO SMALL

 OR

WEAR SHOES THAT ARE
ONE SIZE TOO LARGE?

WOULD YOU RATHER?

7 YEAR OLD
VERSION

PLAYER 1

(ASK THE OTHER PLAYER(S) TO
CHOOSE QUESTION 1 OR QUESTION 2)

A

WOULD YOU RATHER

GET TO LIVE IN A HOUSE
WHERE THE FLOORS
WERE LIKE A BOUNCY
CASTLE

LIVE IN A HOUSE WITH
WATER SLIDES?

B

WOULD YOU RATHER

EVERYONE YOU EVER SEE
SAYS HELLO TO YOU

NO ONE EVER SAYS
HELLO TO YOU?

WOULD YOU RATHER?

7 YEAR OLD
VERSION

PLAYER 2

(ASK THE OTHER PLAYER(S) TO
CHOOSE QUESTION 1 OR QUESTION 2)

A

WOULD YOU RATHER

EAT WHENEVER YOU WANT

 OR

SLEEP WHENEVER YOU WANT?

B

WOULD YOU RATHER

BE GIVEN THE CHANCE TO BE RICH AND FAMOUS

 OR

SPEND YOUR LIFE RICH AND UNKNOWN?

WOULD YOU RATHER?

7 YEAR OLD
VERSION

PLAYER 1

(ASK THE OTHER PLAYER(S) TO
CHOOSE QUESTION 1 OR QUESTION 2)

A · WOULD YOU RATHER

EAT CABBAGE COVERED
IN CHOCOLATE

CHOCOLATE WRAPPED IN
CABBAGE?

B · WOULD YOU RATHER

WATCH A FILM ABOUT
YOUR OWN LIFE

APPEAR IN A FILM
ABOUT SOMEONE ELSE'S
LIFE?

WOULD YOU RATHER?

7 YEAR OLD
VERSION

PLAYER 2

(ASK THE OTHER PLAYER(S) TO
CHOOSE QUESTION 1 OR QUESTION 2)

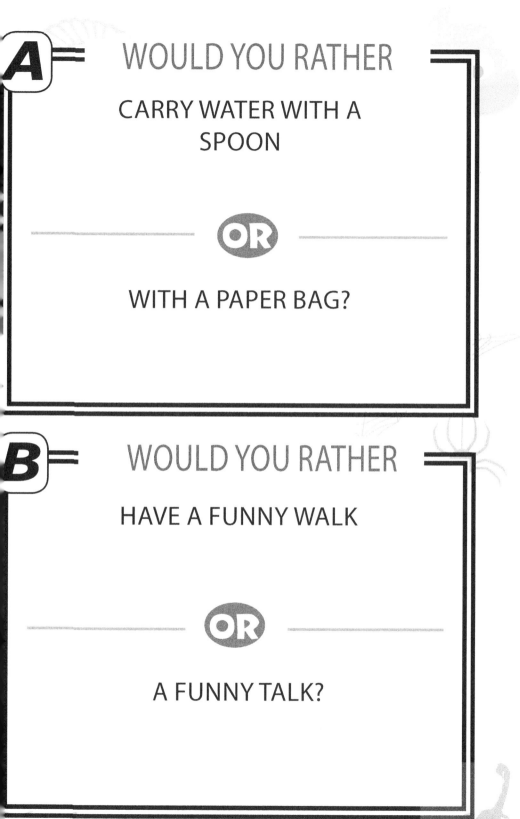

WOULD YOU RATHER?

7 YEAR OLD
VERSION

PLAYER 1

(ASK THE OTHER PLAYER(S) TO
CHOOSE QUESTION 1 OR QUESTION 2)

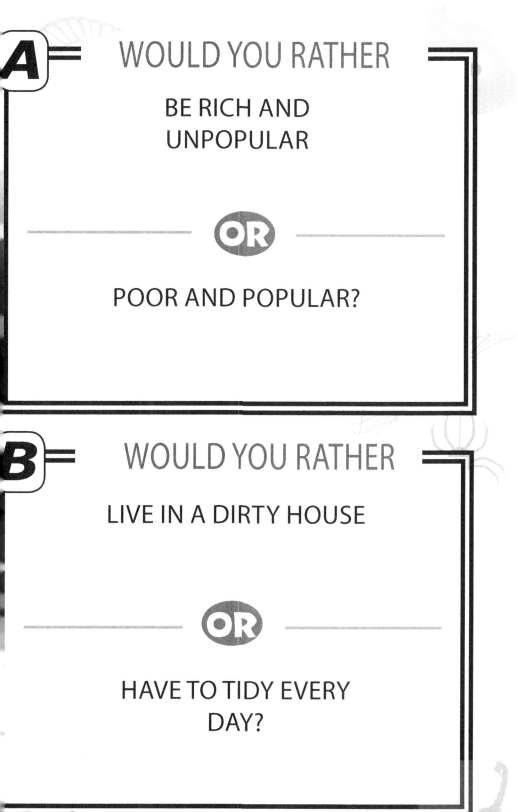

A

WOULD YOU RATHER

BE RICH AND UNPOPULAR

OR

POOR AND POPULAR?

B

WOULD YOU RATHER

LIVE IN A DIRTY HOUSE

OR

HAVE TO TIDY EVERY DAY?

WOULD YOU RATHER?

7 YEAR OLD
VERSION

PLAYER 2

(ASK THE OTHER PLAYER(S) TO
CHOOSE QUESTION 1 OR QUESTION 2)

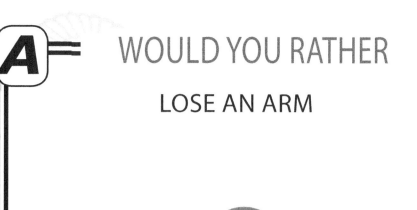

WOULD YOU RATHER

LOSE AN ARM

OR

LOSE A LEG?

WOULD YOU RATHER

RUN A MILE EVERY MORNING

OR

HAVE TO SPEND AN EXTRA HOUR AT SCHOOL EVERY DAY?

WOULD YOU RATHER?

7 YEAR OLD
VERSION

PLAYER 1

(ASK THE OTHER PLAYER(S) TO
CHOOSE QUESTION 1 OR QUESTION 2)

A   WOULD YOU RATHER

GO TO SCHOOL EVERY WEEKEND

 OR

HAVE AN EXTRA HOUR AT SCHOOL EVERY MORNING?

B   WOULD YOU RATHER

BE UNABLE TO YOUR MOUTH

 OR

NOT BE ABLE TO OPEN YOUR EYES?

WOULD YOU RATHER?

7 YEAR OLD
VERSION

PLAYER 1

(ASK THE OTHER PLAYER(S) TO
CHOOSE QUESTION 1 OR QUESTION 2)

A

WOULD YOU RATHER

BE GIVEN A DOG THAT
ACTS LIKE A CAT AS A
PET

A CAT THAT ACTS LIKE A
DOG?

B

WOULD YOU RATHER

BE UNABLE TO GET OUT
OF A ROOM WITH A
CRYING BABY

A BARKING DOG?

WOULD YOU RATHER?

7 YEAR OLD
VERSION

PLAYER 1

(ASK THE OTHER PLAYER(S) TO
CHOOSE QUESTION 1 OR QUESTION 2)

A

WOULD YOU RATHER

SKIP A CLASS AT
SCHOOL EVERY DAY

WATCH AS MUCH TV AS
YOU WANT EVERY DAY?

B

WOULD YOU RATHER

BE ABLE TO LIVE
FOREVER

TRAVEL THROUGH TIME?

WOULD YOU RATHER?

7 YEAR OLD
VERSION

PLAYER 2

(ASK THE OTHER PLAYER(S) TO
CHOOSE QUESTION 1 OR QUESTION 2)

A WOULD YOU RATHER

WIN THE LOTTERY

WIN AN OLYMPIC GOLD MEDAL?

B WOULD YOU RATHER

YOUR HEAD WAS THE SIZE OF A GRAPE

A HEAD THE SIZE OF A PUMPKIN?

WOULD YOU RATHER?

7 YEAR OLD
VERSION

PLAYER 2

(ASK THE OTHER PLAYER(S) TO
CHOOSE QUESTION 1 OR QUESTION 2)

A
WOULD YOU RATHER

WEAR YOUR SHIRT
BACKWARD

WEAR YOUR PANTS
BACKWARD?

B
WOULD YOU RATHER

IT WAS YOUR JOB TO
CLEAN THE TOILETS
EVERY DAY

SORT THROUGH THE
RUBBISH EVERY DAY?

WOULD YOU RATHER?

7 YEAR OLD
VERSION

PLAYER 2

(ASK THE OTHER PLAYER(S) TO
CHOOSE QUESTION 1 OR QUESTION 2)

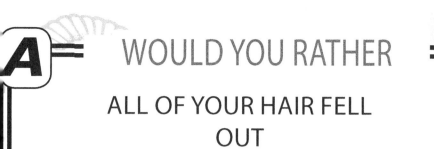

WOULD YOU RATHER

ALL OF YOUR HAIR FELL OUT

ALL YOUR TEETH?

WOULD YOU RATHER

HAVE TO SIT DOWN WITH NO ENTERTAINMENT

STAND UP TO WATCH A FILM?

WOULD YOU RATHER?

7 YEAR OLD
VERSION

PLAYER 1

(ASK THE OTHER PLAYER(S) TO
CHOOSE QUESTION 1 OR QUESTION 2)

A

WOULD YOU RATHER

FIGHT OFF TWO RACCOONS

FIFTY WASPS?

B

WOULD YOU RATHER

SPEND A DAY AT SCHOOL DRESSED AS A CLOWN

IN YOUR SWIMMING COSTUME?

WOULD YOU RATHER?

7 YEAR OLD
VERSION

PLAYER 2

(ASK THE OTHER PLAYER(S) TO
CHOOSE QUESTION 1 OR QUESTION 2)

A

WOULD YOU RATHER

ONLY EAT HOT FOODS ALL SUMMER

EAT COLD FOODS ALL WINTER?

B

WOULD YOU RATHER

BE GIVEN THE ABILITY TO SEE THE FUTURE

READ OTHER PEOPLES' MINDS?

WOULD YOU RATHER?

7 YEAR OLD
VERSION

PLAYER 1

(ASK THE OTHER PLAYER(S) TO
CHOOSE QUESTION 1 OR QUESTION 2)

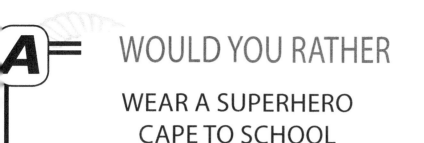

WOULD YOU RATHER

A

WEAR A SUPERHERO CAPE TO SCHOOL

 OR

A PIRATE COSTUME?

B

WOULD YOU RATHER

BE PART OF THE CREW ON A PIRATE SHIP

 OR

ON A SPACE SHIP?

WOULD YOU RATHER?

7 YEAR OLD
VERSION

PLAYER 2

(ASK THE OTHER PLAYER(S) TO
CHOOSE QUESTION 1 OR QUESTION 2)

WOULD YOU RATHER

A

SIT DOWN TO EAT AN ENTIRE CAKE

 OR

EAT A WHOLE CARTON OF ICE CREAM?

WOULD YOU RATHER

B

EAT A SQUASHED SNAIL

 OR

DRINK A BUG SMOOTHIE?

WOULD YOU RATHER?

7 YEAR OLD
VERSION

PLAYER 1

(ASK THE OTHER PLAYER(S) TO
CHOOSE QUESTION 1 OR QUESTION 2)

A | WOULD YOU RATHER

WATCH YOUR FAVORITE CARTOONS ALL NIGHT

 OR

MISS A DAY OF SCHOOL?

B | WOULD YOU RATHER

GO TO HOGWARTS

 OR

GO TO ASTRONAUT SCHOOL?

WOULD YOU RATHER?

7 YEAR OLD
VERSION

PLAYER 2

(ASK THE OTHER PLAYER(S) TO
CHOOSE QUESTION 1 OR QUESTION 2)

A

WOULD YOU RATHER

SNEEZE CHEESE

 OR

COUGH UP CHOCOLATE MILK?

B

WOULD YOU RATHER

BE TOLD THAT YOU CAN CLIMB UP A TREE

 OR

SWIM IN THE SEA?

WOULD YOU RATHER?

7 YEAR OLD
VERSION

PLAYER 1

(ASK THE OTHER PLAYER(S) TO
CHOOSE QUESTION 1 OR QUESTION 2)

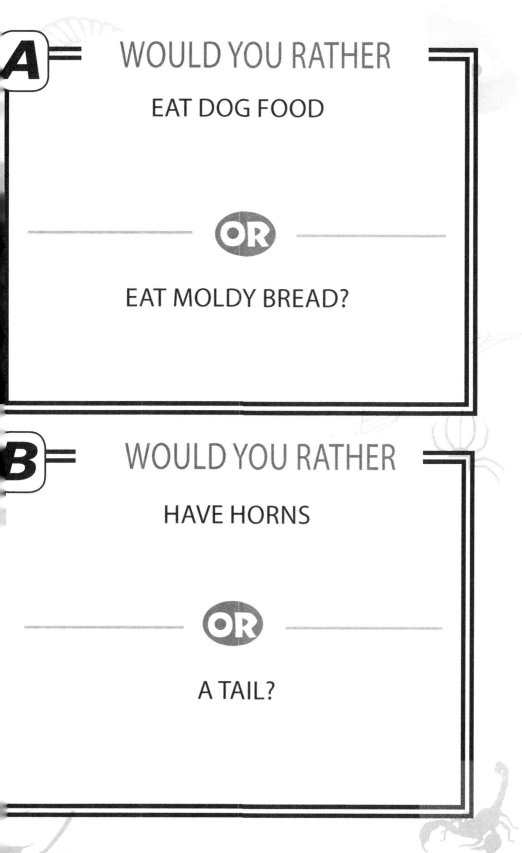

WOULD YOU RATHER

A

EAT DOG FOOD

OR

EAT MOLDY BREAD?

B

WOULD YOU RATHER

HAVE HORNS

OR

A TAIL?

WOULD YOU RATHER?

7 YEAR OLD
VERSION

PLAYER 2

(ASK THE OTHER PLAYER(S) TO
CHOOSE QUESTION 1 OR QUESTION 2)

A

WOULD YOU RATHER

BE ABLE TO PLAY YOUR FAVORITE VIDEO GAME FOR ONE HOUR A DAY

PLAY A DIFFERENT GAME FOR TWO HOURS A DAY?

B

WOULD YOU RATHER

HAVE A PIG'S NOSE

AN ELEPHANT'S TRUNK?

PLAYER 1

(ASK THE OTHER PLAYER(S) TO
CHOOSE QUESTION 1 OR QUESTION 2)

A

WOULD YOU RATHER

SING WHEN YOU TALK

RAP WHEN YOU TALK?

B

WOULD YOU RATHER

HAVE TO HIDE IN YOUR OWN COUNTRY

LIVE IN ANOTHER COUNTRY?

WOULD YOU RATHER?

7 YEAR OLD
VERSION

PLAYER 2

(ASK THE OTHER PLAYER(S) TO
CHOOSE QUESTION 1 OR QUESTION 2)

A

WOULD YOU RATHER

HAVE THE ABILITY TO ALWAYS SEE ONE MINUTE IN THE FUTURE

BE ABLE TO SEE A YEAR IN THE FUTURE ONCE A YEAR?

B

WOULD YOU RATHER

HAVE LONGER SCHOOL DAYS

GO TO SCHOOL ALL YEAR?

WOULD YOU RATHER?

7 YEAR OLD
VERSION

PLAYER 1

(ASK THE OTHER PLAYER(S) TO
CHOOSE QUESTION 1 OR QUESTION 2)

A

WOULD YOU RATHER

BE BANNED FROM EVER
EATING PIZZA AGAIN

 OR

NEVER BE ALLOWED TO
EAT ICE CREAM AGAIN?

B

WOULD YOU RATHER

LIVE A LIFE IN YOUR
FAVORITE MOVIE

 OR

LIVE IN YOUR FAVORITE
TV SHOW?

WOULD YOU RATHER?

7 YEAR OLD
VERSION

PLAYER 2

(ASK THE OTHER PLAYER(S) TO
CHOOSE QUESTION 1 OR QUESTION 2)

A

WOULD YOU RATHER

BE A SUPERHERO WHO IS BAD AT THE JOB

 OR

A SUPERVILLAIN WHO IS VERY GOOD AT THE JOB?

B

WOULD YOU RATHER

BE ABLE TO LIE TO EVERYONE

 OR

BE ABLE TO TELL WHEN OTHER PEOPLE ARE LYING?

PLAYER 1

(ASK THE OTHER PLAYER(S) TO
CHOOSE QUESTION 1 OR QUESTION 2)

WOULD YOU RATHER

GO TO OTHER PLANETS

MEET AN ALIEN?

WOULD YOU RATHER

GO AWAY ON A ROAD TRIP

STAY IN A HOTEL?

WOULD YOU RATHER?

7 YEAR OLD
VERSION

PLAYER 2

(ASK THE OTHER PLAYER(S) TO
CHOOSE QUESTION 1 OR QUESTION 2)

WOULD YOU RATHER

A

BE ABLE TO PLAY IN THE SNOW

OR

SIT BY A FIRE?

WOULD YOU RATHER

B

WATCH FIREWORKS

OR

BUILD A SNOWMAN?

WOULD YOU RATHER?

7 YEAR OLD
VERSION

PLAYER 1

(ASK THE OTHER PLAYER(S) TO
CHOOSE QUESTION 1 OR QUESTION 2)

A. WOULD YOU RATHER

HAVE TO DANCE INSTEAD OF WALK

 OR

HOP INSTEAD OF WALK?

B. WOULD YOU RATHER

BE ABLE TO HAVE YOUR OWN ROBOT

 OR

YOUR OWN DINOSAUR?

WOULD YOU RATHER?

7 YEAR OLD
VERSION

PLAYER 2

(ASK THE OTHER PLAYER(S) TO
CHOOSE QUESTION 1 OR QUESTION 2)

A

WOULD YOU RATHER

HAVE THE ABILITY TO COOK ANYTHING YOU WANTED

BE ABLE TO SING ANY SONG?

B

WOULD YOU RATHER

WALK TO SCHOOL WITH YOUR FRIENDS

GET A LIFT TO SCHOOL IN A CAR ON YOUR OWN?

WOULD YOU RATHER?

7 YEAR OLD
VERSION

PLAYER 1

(ASK THE OTHER PLAYER(S) TO
CHOOSE QUESTION 1 OR QUESTION 2)

A

WOULD YOU RATHER

PUT TOO MUCH KETCHUP ON A HOTDOG

TOO MANY ONIONS?

B

WOULD YOU RATHER

HAVE UNLIMITED MONEY

SUPERPOWERS?

WOULD YOU RATHER?

7 YEAR OLD
VERSION

PLAYER 2

(ASK THE OTHER PLAYER(S) TO
CHOOSE QUESTION 1 OR QUESTION 2)

A

WOULD YOU RATHER

HAVE A TAP WITH RUNNING CHOCOLATE MILK

AN OVEN THAT IS ALWAYS FULL OF HOT PIZZA?

B

WOULD YOU RATHER

BE ABLE TO LEARN TO SURF

LEARN TO RIDE A HORSE?

Made in the USA
Monee, IL
01 March 2023

28951876R10057